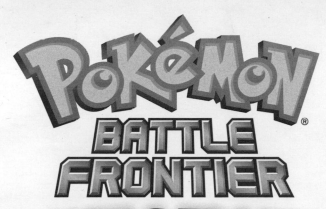

GROVYLE TROUBLE

Based on the episode "Odd Pokémon Out"

ADAPTED BY TRACEY WEST

110645250

SCHOLASTIC INC.

New York   Toronto   London   Auckland   Sydney
Mexico City   New Delhi   Hong Kong   Buenos Aires

No part of this publication may be reproduced, stored in a retrieval system, or transmitted in any form or by any
means, electronic, mechanical, photocopying, recording, or otherwise, without written permission of the publisher.
For information regarding permission, write to Scholastic Inc., Attention: Permissions Department, 557 Broadway,
New York, NY 10012.

ISBN-13: 978-0-545-10561-3
ISBN-10: 0-545-10561-7

12 11 10 9 8 7 6 5 4 3 2 1   8 9 10 11 12/0

Designed by Cheung Tai
Printed in the U.S.A.

First printing, September 2008

Stampede!

Ash Ketchum looked over the ship's rails. His Pokémon, Pikachu, sat on his shoulder. Blue water sparkled below. A flock of Wingull flew in the clear sky overhead.

"Look! It's Chamomile Island!" May cried.

She sounded nervous, and Ash knew why. Ash and his friends May, Max, and Brock were exploring the Battle Frontier. May entered her Pokémon in contests whenever she could. She wanted to win a ribbon at each Contest Hall.

The next one was on Chrysanthemum Island. To get there, they'd have to board a connecting ship on Chamomile Island.

"Don't worry, May," Ash said. "We'll get there in time for the contest."

The ship docked soon after. The friends had some time before the next connecting ship came. They left the dock and gazed out onto the grassy plains of Chamomile Island.

The place was a real haven for wild Pokémon. Yellow and brown Girafarig peacefully munched on grass. Ponyta raced across the plains, their fiery manes flaming behind them.

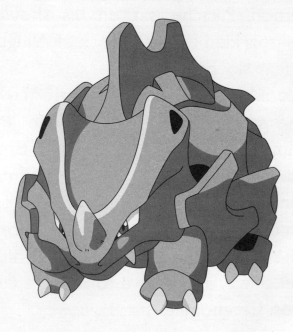

"Awesome, a herd of Rhyhorn!" Max said, pointing. Behind his glasses, his dark eyes shone with excitement.

Ash had never seen so many Rhyhorn together in one place. The tough-looking Pokémon had thick, gray skin. Each one had a sharp horn on top of its nose, and jagged ridges sticking out from its body.

"There are all kinds of Pokémon out here," Brock said, looking around.

That gave Ash an idea. "Hey, let's bring the gang out for some fun!"

"All right!" May agreed.

Ash, May, and Brock tossed out the Poké Balls they were carrying. Their Pokémon appeared in bright flashes of light.

Ash's Donphan, Corphish, Grovyle, and Swellow popped out.

Brock's Forretress, Marshtomp, and Bonsly joined them.

Then came May's Pokémon: Munchlax, Squirtle, Eevee, and Combusken.

Ash's Pikachu never traveled in a Poké Ball. The little yellow Pokémon hopped off Ash's shoulder and ran to join its friends.

With a happy cry, the Pokémon scattered across the plains.

Donphan ran up a tiny hill. The Armor Pokémon had two sharp tusks, and a thick trunk. Donphan looked tough, but had a playful personality.

Three baby Rhyhorn ran up the hill, pushing a ball made of grass. The ball rolled toward Donphan. It happily picked up the ball with its

trunk. Then it ran toward the Rhyhorn. Donphan wanted to play catch!

But the little Rhyhorn got scared. They turned and ran. Donphan didn't know they were scared, so it ran after them to play.

Then two *big* Rhyhorn charged up the hill. Their eyes glowed red with anger. They thought Donphan wanted to hurt their babies.

Surprised, Donphan skidded to a stop. The ball dropped from its trunk. Donphan spun around and ran away as fast as it could.

More Rhyhorn gave chase. Soon the ground rumbled as their heavy feet pounded the ground.

Ash felt the ground shake. He looked up and saw Donphan running toward him.

Then he saw the charging herd of Rhyhorn.

The others saw it too.

"Stampede!" they yelled.

Grovyle vs. Tropius

A loud car engine drowned out the sound of the stampede. Ash saw a jeep speeding toward them. The jeep cleared the top of a hill. Then it landed between Ash and the Rhyhorn herd.

Dust clouds puffed from under the jeep's tires. Nurse Joy jumped out. She faced the herd and threw a Poké Ball into the air.

"Meganium, let's go!" she yelled.

A green Pokémon burst from the ball. Big pink flower petals grew around its neck, like a collar. The Pokémon's thick body rested on four sturdy legs. It had a long neck, and two thin antennae waved on top of its forehead like thin flower stems.

"Ganium!" it cried.

"Meganium, use Growl now!" Nurse Joy ordered.

Meganium nodded and opened its wide mouth. An eerie sound came forth, traveling on sonic waves.

Growl hit the Rhyhorn herd. They all sank to the ground. It put them to sleep immediately.

The stampede was over.

Nurse Joy turned to Ash and his friends. "Everyone okay?"

"Thanks to you, Nurse Joy," Ash answered, smiling. Ash had traveled all over the world, and everywhere he went he saw Nurse Joy or one of her sisters. They all had pink hair and wore white uniforms. "You two were great!"

May admired Nurse Joy's Pokémon. "Wow, a Meganium," she said.

Ash flipped on his Pokédex and typed quickly.

Meganium's picture appeared on the small screen.

"Meganium, the Herb Pokémon," the Pokédex said. "Meganium's breath has the power to revive dead grass and plants. The fragrance emanating from its flower petals can soothe angry, hostile emotions."

Meganium smiled sweetly. *"Ganium!"* the Pokémon said.

Brock rushed toward Nurse Joy. He had a dreamy look in his eyes.

"Nurse Joy, you are just like Meganium," he told her. "Your ravishing beauty and gentle nature is like a refreshing breeze that blows calmly across these plains!"

Max frowned. Why did Brock have to fall in love with every female who crossed his path? He grabbed Brock by the ear.

"Too bad for you I've kept *my* anger and hostility," he said, pulling Brock away.

Nurse Joy smiled at Ash. "You've got quite a group of Pokémon there," she said. "I do hope they're feeling all right."

"Thanks!" Ash said. He scanned the Pokémon. They all looked calm after the Rhyhorn scare. "Everything looks fine to me!"

Then Ash noticed something. His Grovyle was missing!

"Hold on! Where did Grovyle go?" he asked.

Pikachu pointed to a nearby apple tree. Ash's green Grovyle stood there. Grovyle stood almost three feet tall. It had a sleek, green body with a pink underbelly. Long, green leaves grew from its wrists, the top of its head, and its tail. A brown stick dangled from its mouth. Its yellow eyes burned with determination.

A big, brown Pokémon faced Grovyle. It was more than twice the size of Grovyle, with a solid lower body and a long, thick neck. A green leaf covered the top of its head like some kind of helmet. Yellow fruit dangled from the Pokémon's

neck. Large green leaves grew out of its back. They looked like wings.

"What's going on?" Ash asked. "And who's the other guy?"

He flipped open his Pokédex.

"Tropius. The Fruit Pokémon," the Pokédex reported. "The fruit that grows around its neck is sweet and popular with children. It flies by flapping the large leaves on its body."

Ash frowned. Tropius sounded like a friendly Pokémon. But *this* Tropius was a lot bigger than Grovyle — and it looked really angry.

"Ganium." Meganium sounded worried.

"Oh no!" Nurse Joy cried. "It looks like Tropius has taken over that tree as its own. So if anyone dares to come close, Tropius attacks!"

"Whoa, that's awful!" Ash wailed.

Before Ash could do anything to help Grovyle, Tropius leaped into the air. It smacked Grovyle with its wings, knocking the Grass-type Pokémon to the ground.

Grovyle jumped to its feet. But Tropius was

flapping its wings now, getting ready for a new attack.

"Grovyle, look out!" Ash warned.

Whoosh! Tropius blasted Grovyle with a powerful Gust attack. The wind sent Grovyle tumbling backward.

"Hold on, I'm coming!" Ash cried. He ran toward the tree, but the strong winds pushed him back.

Before Grovyle could recover, Tropius attacked with Razor Leaf. The sharp leaves stung Grovyle's body.

"Meganium, stop Tropius!" Nurse Joy commanded.

"Ganium!" The Pokémon nodded and then jumped into the air. It used Razor Leaf, too. The attack stunned the unexpecting Tropius.

Meganium ran up to Tropius. The big Pokémon hung its head. It looked ashamed.

"Ganium, Ganium, Ganium!" Meganium scolded.

"Wow!" Max remarked. "Meganium just stopped Tropius dead in its tracks!"

Team Rocket's Plot

"I've seen this before," Nurse Joy said. "For some reason, Tropius won't attack my Meganium."

Ash ran to his Pokémon. "Grovyle! Grovyle!"

The Pokémon lay in the grass, flat on its back. Its eyes were closed.

"Say something, Grovyle, please!" Ash begged.

The Pokémon's eyes fluttered. *"Gro ... vyle,"* it said weakly.

Ash's friends and Nurse Joy gathered around.

"No time to lose!" Nurse Joy said. "We've

got to get Grovyle to the Pokémon Center right away!"

Ash carried Grovyle to Nurse Joy's jeep. Everyone piled in. Then the car quickly sped away.

Tropius watched them go. It looked sad to see Meganium leave. It sighed, then began to munch apples from the tree.

Three figures watched Tropius from a nearby bush.

One was a young woman with long, magenta hair. She wore a white uniform with a red "R" on the front.

The second was a young man with bluish hair. He wore a white uniform, too.

The third was a small white Pokemon with big eyes, whiskers, and pointy brown and black ears. An oval gold jewel sat in the center of its forehead.

It was Team Rocket, of course — a trio of Pokémon thieves.

"Talk about brawn," Jessie said, admiring Tropius.

"Bravo! Tropius is feisty *and* fruit-filled," James agreed.

"Which means, it's a perfect present for the Boss!" Meowth added.

Jessie and James were shocked. "Have you flipped your script?"

"Not yet," Meowth said. "Keep what's left of your minds open and dig this!"

Meowth got a dreamy look in its eyes. It imagined Team Rocket's boss relaxing on a beach.

"Imagine the Boss lazin' around on some island under the shade of those large leaves growing out of Tropius's back," Meowth said. "And while he's being fanned by Tropius's leaves, the Boss could take a little pause for the cause by chowing down on some of Tropius's yummy fruit. And remembering who made it all possible, guess what he's gonna say?"

Meowth beamed. "He's going to say, 'Excellent! I've got to reward Meowth and his friends with a big promotion and a fat raise!'"

Jessie and James got caught up in Meowth's fantasy.

"We've been lumped up," James said.

"Now we're getting bumped up," Jessie added.

"To first class!" the two cheered together.

Jessie's eyes focused on Tropius. "Now all we have to do is log and capture."

Meowth frowned. It remembered the powerful attacks Tropius used on Grovyle. "That's easier said than done."

"Wait! Perhaps a dab of diplomacy might do the deed," James suggested.

Jessie nodded. "You're a dandy, double-talking diplomat, Meowth."

"Me? No way!" Meowth cried.

"Yes way!" James said. "Talk to Tropius. With your natural negotiating skills, it'll be eating out of your paw."

"Either that, or *eating* my paw," Meowth

mumbled. It sighed. Jessie and James wouldn't let Meowth back out now.

Seconds later, Meowth tiptoed up to Tropius. It used a megaphone so it wouldn't have to get too close.

"Uh, my name is Meowth, Team Rocket negotiator," Meowth announced. Tropius stopped munching on an apple. It looked at Meowth curiously.

"Have I got a sweet deal for you!" Meowth went on. "How'd you like anything you ever wanted? All the Pokémon food you can eat? A pillow for that big head of yours? If it exists and you want it, I can get it!"

"Eeee?" Tropius squeaked. It was definitely interested.

Tropius and Meowth talked for a little while. Jessie and James waited anxiously. They watched Meowth nod at Tropius.

"No problemo!" Meowth told Tropius. "I'm a can-do Pokémon and you can consider it done, dude!"

Meowth walked back to Jessie and James.

"So what does Tropius want?" James asked.

"Tropius just wants Meganium to come along, too," Meowth announced.

"What?!" Jessie and James were shocked.

"Tropius and Meganium are in love," Meowth explained.

"*Eeeee*," Tropius blushed.

"That would totally explain why Tropius stopped attacking just as soon as Meganium made the scene," Jessie realized.

"Rumor has it that Meganium have the power to heal," James said. "So if we were to gift the Boss with a package deal ..."

"I can hear his happy squeal!" Jessie finished.

Meowth's eyes glittered at the thought of bringing *two* Pokémon to the Boss.

"Let's stop rappin' and make it real!" Meowth cried.

Grovyle in Love

Nurse Joy sped to the nearby Pokémon Center. There, Trainers could find shelter, meet other trainers, and heal their injured Pokémon.

Soon Grovyle was resting on a bed in a clean, white room. Nurse Joy, Ash, and the others surrounded the Pokémon. Meganium leaned over the bed and opened its mouth wide.

Meganium's sweet, healing breath wafted over Grovyle. The sound of soothing chimes filled the air, and a soft white light lit up the room. Grovyle immediately looked calmer and more relaxed.

"Nurse Joy, do you think Grovyle will be all right?" Ash asked, worried.

"Pikachu?" Pikachu was worried, too.

"I think so," Nurse Joy replied. "Meganium's healing powers should be strong enough to deal with Grovyle's wounds."

Grovyle opened its eyes. *"Grovyle,"* it said weakly.

Meganium smiled happily. *"Ganium!"*

Grovyle's cheeks turned red. Then something amazing happened. A flower bloomed on the end of the stick in Grovyle's mouth!

"Grovyle?" Ash asked.

"You see?" May said. "All this attention from Meganium and Grovyle's better already."

"Maybe, but it looks more like true love to me," Brock said.

Grovyle hid its face, embarrassed.

"Grovyle's going to be fine," Nurse Joy assured them. "Things will be back to normal after a bit more rest. For now, take it easy, Grovyle!"

Nurse Joy left the room, and Meganium followed her.

"Thanks, both of you!" Ash called after them.

Grovyle's face flushed as it watched Meganium walk away. Ash looked at Grovyle, concerned.

"Guys, check it out!" Ash told his friends. "Grovyle's burning up!"

"It's a fever," Brock whispered to Max and May. "A fever Grovyle got from being *love* sick!"

"Poor thing," May said. "I guess it's better than being banged up!"

"But after losing to Tropius in the first place, it didn't exactly help to build up Grovyle's confidence," Brock reminded them. "Talk about being embarrassed — no wonder Grovyle's feeling frustrated about telling Meganium its true feelings!"

May nodded. "That would explain a lot."

"After all of that, no wonder Grovyle's feeling so bad," Max added.

Ash knew how Grovyle must feel. But there wasn't much they could do for the Pokémon now. "Grovyle needs lots of sleep," Ash told his friends.

"The best thing we can do is let Grovyle rest," Brock agreed.

"Right," Ash said. "A little down time and Grovyle will be good as new!"

Ash, Brock, May, and Max left the room. Grovyle sat up in bed.

It didn't want to rest at all.

It wanted to face Tropius again!

Ash and the others walked through the halls of the Pokémon Center. Then they heard a cry.

"Meganium!" Nurse Joy shouted.

They took off running and he found Nurse Joy standing by a hole in the wall of the Pokémon Center. Something had busted right through!

"Nurse Joy, what happened?" Ash asked.

Nurse Joy looked frantic. "They stole Meganium!"

She pointed outside to where a giant metal robot towered over the Pokémon Center. It walked on two giant, metal legs and had two dangerous claws at the end of its long, metal arms. Meganium was trapped in one of the claws!

"Yeah, but who are they?" Ash wondered.

The top of the robot opened up. Jessie and James popped out.

"Prepare for trouble as we give you a peek!" Jessie said.

"And make it double, aren't I a sneak?" James asked.

Meowth popped up next. "With Meowth —"

it began, but James's Mime Jr. interrupted it. It hopped right in front of Meowth's face!

"Mime mime mime!" the cute pink Pokémon chanted.

Team Rocket continued its motto.

"Whenever there's peace in the universe ..." Jessie began.

"Team Rocket ..." James continued.

"Is there ..." Meowth tried to finish, but Mime Jr. jumped in front of it again.

"Mime mime mime mime mime!" it cried happily.

"Wobbuffet!" Jessie's big, blue Pokémon chimed in.

Meowth was fuming. "Do that again and you'll be cute and *flat!*" Meowth warned Mime Jr.

Ash wasn't amused by any of these antics.

"Team Rocket!" he cried angrily, clenching his fists.

"Show's over!" Jessie said quickly. The lid to the robot closed. Then the robot stomped away across the island.

Ash broke into a run.

"Come on, hurry!" Brock yelled, running after him.

"Right!" Max and May agreed.

They chased after the robot.

They had to save Meganium!

The Rematch Begins

Grovyle didn't know that Meganium had been kidnapped. The Grass-type Pokémon had one thing on its mind. It wanted to beat Tropius in battle. Grovyle knew it was the only way it could face Meganium again.

Grovyle raced back to the apple tree. Tropius and Grovyle faced off once again.

"*Grovyle*," Grovyle challenged.

"*Eeeee*," Tropius replied in a low growl.

"*Grovyle*." Grovyle wanted Tropius to know it meant business.

"*Eeeee*." Tropius was ready to rumble.

Tropius made the first move. It flapped its

large wings. A powerful Gust attack swept toward Grovyle.

"*Gro!*" The attack sent Grovyle flying.

Tropius didn't let up. *Wham!* It pummeled Grovyle with Razor Leaf.

Grovyle shielded its face from the sharp, flying leaves. It was just like before. It didn't stand a chance against Tropius....

Then, from the corner of its eye, Grovyle saw the flower on the end of the stick. It remembered Meganium's sweet face.

That was all Grovyle needed. It jumped to its feet, and raced across the grass so quickly that Tropius didn't even see it.

Tropius stopped, confused. Where had Grovyle gone? Tropius flew through the air, looking for its opponent.

Grovyle jumped up onto a high tree branch. It watched Tropius down below.

Then, *bam!* Grovyle hit Tropius with a Bullet Seed attack. The move caught Tropius off guard. The big Pokémon stumbled.

Slash! Grovyle attacked next with Fury Cutter.
Tropius fell to the ground. Then it fainted.

"Gro!" Grovyle cried triumphantly.

Then Grovyle heard a sing-song voice. "Tropius!
We're home!"

Team Rocket's giant robot stomped up to the
tree. The mechanical arm lowered Meganium to
the ground.

"We brought Meganium, just like we
promised!" Meowth called out.

"Gro?" Grovyle was confused.

So was Team Rocket.

"Hold on!" Jessie cried. "Isn't that Grovyle from the twerp's troops?"

"And why isn't Tropius jumping for joy at our return?" James wondered.

"Looks like *Tropius* got jumped instead!" Meowth remarked.

"Ganium!" A worried Meganium ran toward the tree.

Grovyle's heart began to thump. Was Meganium running toward Grovyle? It had to be true love!

Meganium ran up to Grovyle. Grovyle's cheeks burned red. It held out its arms . . .

But Meganium ran past Grovyle. It stopped next to Tropius.

"Ganium!"

"Troooo," Tropius said weakly. It couldn't lift its head.

"Ganium." A white, sparkling light shone from Meganium. The light showered Tropius.

The big Grass-and-Flying-type Pokémon felt

better. It got to its feet. Then it smiled at Meganium.

"*Troooo*," it said, thanking Meganium.

"*Ganium!*" Meganium was very happy. The two Pokémon gently rubbed heads.

"You know, not that it matters, but don't they look kind of sweet?" Jessie said.

"Too sweet!" Meowth agreed. "Matter of fact, those two love birds go together like ketchup and fries!"

James gazed over at Grovyle. The green Pokémon hung its head sadly.

"Poor Grovyle," James remarked. "Another victim of the heart."

"Grovyle!" the poor Pokémon wailed. Grovyle fell to its knees. The flower on the end of its stick wilted and died.

Nurse Joy's jeep sped onto the scene. The jeep stopped, squealing on its brakes.

Ash jumped out of the car first. He saw his Pokémon lying on the ground.

"Oh no! Grovyle!" Ash cried.

An Amazing Evolution

Ash angrily glared up at Team Rocket.

"What happened?" he yelled. "What did you do to Grovyle?"

"*Pika!*" Pikachu added.

"Don't look at us!" James protested. "That's not our style."

"That was the by-product of a little bit of fisticuffs between Grovyle and Tropius," Meowth added.

Ash shook his head. "Oh man!" he exclaimed. He turned to Grovyle. "So you wanted to prove you could beat Tropius and ended up losing."

"Wake up!" Meowth cried, annoyed. "Can't

you see Grovyle beat the leaves off of Tropius, twerp?"

Ash was surprised. "Yeah? So why does Grovyle look so bummed out?"

Brock knew the answer. "It's obvious! Grovyle won the game of battle . . . but lost the game of love."

"He won *and* he lost? How do you figure that?" Ash sighed. "Brock, you've got to learn how to make up your mind."

Brock looked at Max and May and shrugged. Sometimes Ash just didn't get it.

"Courtship over," Meowth said cheerfully. He pulled a lever on the robot's control panel. "Time to haul in the happy couple!"

The two mechanical arms reached down. One metal claw grabbed Meganium. The other metal claw grabbed Tropius.

"Ganium!"

"Eeeee!"

"Quit your crying," Jessie snapped. "At least you're together!"

"Oh no!" Ash yelled.

"My Meganium!" Nurse Joy cried out.

Grovyle watched as the arm lifted Meganium into the air. The sweet Pokémon struggled to get free.

Grovyle jumped to its feet. It was angry now. It had to save Meganium.

"Grovyle!"

A bright light burst from Grovyle's body. It shimmered. Ash had to shield his eyes from the glow.

Then the light slowly faded. Now Grovyle looked completely different. It was taller, with a more muscular body. Sharp leaves grew from its arms. Its long tail was made of leaves.

"Awesome!" Ash cheered. "Grovyle's evolved into Sceptile!"

A Pokémon Without Punch

Ash checked his Pokédex to find out about his new Pokémon.

"Sceptile, the Forest Pokémon," the Pokédex said. "Its arms are equipped with razor-sharp leaves and it moves lightly through tree branches in order to attack its enemies."

"Sceptile, heads up!" Ash cried. "Go and get Tropius back!"

"*Sceeeeeept!*" Sceptile jumped high in the air, ready to attack the robot.

"We're gonna get creamed!" Meowth yelled.

Jessie and James screamed in panic.

"Seviper! Prepare for battle!" Jessie cried. She threw out a Poké Ball.

"Cacnea, you too!" James joined in. He threw a Poké Ball, too.

Meowth pulled a lever on the controls. "Time for a double dose of dynamite!"

A door on the robot's body slid open. Two Pokémon jumped up.

Seviper had a long, black body with yellow markings. Two long fangs grew from its mouth. Its tail ended in a sharp blade.

Cacnea had a round, green body. Sharp spikes stuck out of its head and its thick arms. Both Pokémon were ready to battle.

Ash made the first move.

"Now, Bullet Seed, Sceptile!" he cried.

Sceptile sprang into action. It jumped up and opened its mouth.

Nothing came out.

"Hey, no Bullet Seed!" Ash said, shocked.

"Is Sceptile sick, too?" Brock wondered.

Ash frowned. "Okay, do Leaf Blade!"

Sceptile jumped up and twirled. Sharp leaves should have flown out of its body. But nothing happened.

"*Scept?*" Sceptile was pretty confused.

Jessie, James, and Meowth burst out laughing.

"That's funny!" Meowth chortled. "I'm worried about Grovyle evolving, but all I get is a wimp!"

"Great!" Jessie said. "Time to kick Seviper up a confidence notch. Poison Tail, go!"

"*Seviper!*" The Poison-type Pokémon leapt up. *Bam!* It bashed Sceptile with its sharp tail.

"*Aaaaah!*" Sceptile moaned.

"Good show!" James cheered. "Cacnea, Needle Arm!"

Wham! Cacnea whacked Sceptile with its spiky arm. Sceptile hit the ground with a thud.

Team Rocket's Pokémon knew Sceptile couldn't fight back.

Wham!

Smack!

Bam!

They attacked Sceptile again and again.

"*Scept . . .*" Sceptile was too weak to move. Meowth grinned. "Now for the punch line!"

It pulled another lever on the controls. The robot's giant leg raised up. It hovered over Sceptile, ready to stomp!

Teamwork

"Pikachu! Aim for that machine's legs!" Ash yelled. "Thunderbolt, now!"

"Pika!" Pikachu cried. It jumped off of Ash's shoulder.

"Pikachuuuuuuuuuuuuuu!"

Pikachu's body burned with electricity. It curled its body into a tight little ball. Then ...

Blam! A sizzling electric charge blasted the robot's legs. The metal legs began to wobble.

"We're weak in the knees!" James said.

The big robot could no longer stand. It fell backwards with a loud crash. The robot's arms swung forward. The metal claws opened up.

Meganium and Tropius jumped safely to the ground.

Nurse Joy ran up to them. "Meganium! Tropius! You're safe!" she said happily.

Team Rocket wasn't so lucky. They tumbled out of the robot's body, dirty and shaken.

"Let's get out of here before something else gets broken," Jessie moaned.

"Good thinking," Meowth agreed. He held up a small remote control device. "Of course, I just happen to be one step ahead of you!"

Meowth pressed a red button on the remote. "Goin' down!" he said.

Team Rocket's balloon floated down from the sky. The balloon had a Meowth face on it.

"Groovy, our ride's here!" James said.

Jessie, James, and Meowth jumped into the balloon basket. Seviper and Cacnea hopped in, too. Then the balloon began to fly away.

"Going up!" Team Rocket cried. "Next stop — not here!"

"Team Rocket, come back!" Ash yelled.

Sceptile stared after the balloon, helpless to stop it.

Tropius and Meganium looked at each other. They nodded.

"Eeeeeee!" Tropius cried. It flew up into the air after the balloon.

"Ganium!" Meganium launched into Razor Leaf attack. The sharp leaves flew up toward the balloon. Then Tropius flapped its wings harder. It used Gust to send the leaves flying higher and faster.

Brock was impressed. "That Razor Leaf actually picked up power from Gust!" he remarked.

The sharp leaves sliced into the balloon. Hot air shot out. The balloon spiraled off into the distance.

"This is getting old!" Jessie complained.

"And we're not getting any younger!" James added.

"We're blasting off again!" Team Rocket shouted.

"*Wobbuffet!*" The blue Pokémon added.

Meganium and Tropius smiled at each other. They put their heads together and nuzzled.

"Those two were amazing together," Max said.

"What a nice couple!" May added.

Sceptile looked sadly at the two Pokémon.

It had done everything it could.

It had beaten Tropius. It had even evolved. But it couldn't save Meganium. It couldn't win Meganium's love.

Sceptile sighed.

It was no fun being the odd Pokémon out!

9

A Hundred Percent

The friends all went back to the Pokémon Center. This time, Tropius came, too. Tropius and Meganium watched the setting sun together.

"They sure look happy together," May remarked.

"Yes, and not only that, they're going to live together at the Pokémon Center," said Nurse Joy. "Isn't that nice?"

"Oh, that's so sweet," May said.

Ash was happy for Tropius and Meganium. But he couldn't stop thinking about Sceptile. After Team Rocket blasted off, he called

Sceptile back into its Poké Ball. Now he stared at the Poké Ball in his hand.

"I'm worried, Nurse Joy," he said. "Do you think Sceptile's gonna be all right?"

"Don't worry, Ash," Nurse Joy said gently. "You see, nothing's wrong with Sceptile."

Ash frowned. "If that's true, how come Sceptile couldn't do any attack moves?"

"I think it had a lot to do with a broken heart," Nurse Joy explained.

"I thought evolving fixed that," Ash said, surprised.

Nurse Joy leaned in toward the Poké Ball. "Tell me, Ash, hasn't Sceptile always been a hard worker when training with you?"

"You bet!" Ash replied. "Sceptile always gives it a hundred percent."

"Good!" Nurse Joy said. "So now you've

learned that it's not always enough to be physically strong, you know?"

Ash wasn't sure he got it.

"There are all sorts of different ways a Pokémon evolves," Nurse Joy explained. "And when you find yourself in a bind, you learn from it and grow and grow, like Sceptile's doing. And as a Trainer, you're going to grow from it, too, right?"

Ash nodded. Grovyle had learned an important lesson about itself. It needed to learn that lesson so it could evolve. Ash knew that as a Trainer, he was always learning new things about himself.

"Right!" Ash said.

"Pika!" Pikachu agreed.

"I thought so," Nurse Joy said. "And meeting good people like you is why I love my job."

Soon it was time to go. Ash, Brock, May, and Max

boarded the ship bound for Chrysanthemum Island. Nurse Joy stood on the dock with Tropius and Meganium. She waved as the ship sailed away.

"Bye Nurse Joy! Thanks a lot!" Ash called out.

"I will," Nurse Joy called back. "And May, good luck with your contest!"

"Thanks!" May answered. "I'll do my best!"

Ash looked down at his Poké Ball and smiled.

Sceptile *always* did its best for Ash. And that's really what mattered.

The ship sailed into the sunset. Ash didn't know what new adventure he would find on Chrysanthemum Island.

But whatever new challenges he faced, he knew he would do his best!

POKÉMON®

BATTLE FRONTIER

DEOXYS IN DANGER

Based on the episode "Deoxys Crisis"

ADAPTED BY TRACEY WEST

SCHOLASTIC INC.

New York   Toronto   London   Auckland   Sydney
Mexico City   New Delhi   Hong Kong   Buenos Aires

ISBN-13: 978-0-545-10561-3
ISBN-10: 0-545-10561-7

12 11 10 9 8 7 6 5 4 3 2 1   8 9 10 11 12/0

Designed by Cheung Tai
Printed in the U.S.A.

First printing, September 2008

The Strange Aurora

Morning sunshine shone on the Kanto region. Ash Ketchum and his friends were walking along a wooded trail.

Everyone was excited about the adventures that awaited them. In the Battle Frontier, Trainers could earn Frontier Symbols.

"The more Pokémon Contests I enter, the better everything gets!" May said. Her blue eyes shone with excitement. "Soon I'll be at the Grand Festival and it's going to be great! Boy, I wish it were happening now!"

May's little brother, Max, rolled his eyes. "After all you just said, you'd be too tired to compete!" he pointed out.

Brock had other things on his mind. "I can't believe I'm finally going back to my old stomping grounds, Pewter City!" he said.

"And after we go there, it's the Battle Pyramid," Ash said. "We're going to raise the roof on that place, aren't we?"

"Pika!" agreed Pikachu. The little yellow Pokémon was perched on Ash's shoulder.

The trail came out onto a cliff overlooking a beautiful mountain range. The mountains' snowy peaks shone white against the blue sky.

"That's awesome," Ash said, taking in the sight.

A flock of Pokémon joined the scene. Altaria flew across the sky. They had bright blue bodies and tiny white beaks. Their blue tails streamed out behind them. But the most striking thing about them were their fluffy white wings. The wings looked almost like clouds.

Among the Altaria were some Swablu. They were much smaller than the Altaria. They had round, blue bodies and white beaks. Their fluffy white wings looked like clouds, too.

"Wonder where they're going?" Brock asked.

Ash waved to the Pokémon. "Hey! You guys be careful!"

The flock flew over the mountaintops. At the same time, white lights shimmered in the sky around them. The lights changed from white to purple to blue, then disappeared.

"Look! It's a gorgeous aurora. Wow!" May said, amazed.

Max frowned. He knew something about auroras. Lights in the sky were a natural phenomenon that happened in certain parts of the world.

He had never heard of an aurora in the Kanto region.

Suddenly, Pikachu's red cheeks began to sparkle with energy.

"Pika pi!" Pikachu grimaced and lowered its head.

"What's wrong, Pikachu?" Ash asked.

"Pika." Pikachu didn't know.

Up in the sky, the Altaria and Swablu began to fly around in strange circles. They seemed to be very confused.

"Whatever just happened must be messing them up," Max guessed.

"And if they keep flying around like that they'll never get anywhere!" Brock said.

Ash had an idea. "Maybe Swellow can lead them in the right direction."

Ash took a Poké Ball from his belt. It held his Flying-type Pokémon.

"Swellow, I choose you!" Ash cried. He pressed the button on the ball.

Normally, Swellow would burst from the ball in a flash of light. But nothing happened.

"It's not working!" Ash said, surprised.

May tried to open one of her Poké Balls. "Mine isn't either."

"Same for me," Brock said. "But why would our Poké Balls be on the blink?"

Max wasn't old enough to be a Pokémon Trainer yet. He didn't have any Poké Balls. But he did have a PokéNav. The handheld device helped Max plan their journey around the Battle Frontier.

Max then tried the PokéNav. "It doesn't work either," he reported.

"Something's making everything short out," Ash realized.

He looked up in the sky, where he had seen the aurora. Then he noticed a figure on a cliff just above them. It was a young woman wearing the uniform of a Pokémon Ranger. She wore gray shorts and tall gray boots. She had a short-sleeved white and red jacket with a gold collar. She wore her light blue hair in a ponytail on top of her head.

A small Pokémon sat on her shoulder. The cream-colored Pokémon had long, red ears. The red cheeks on its happy, round face had plus signs in the middle of them. Even its little red tail was shaped like a plus sign.

"It's Solana, the gorgeous Pokémon Ranger!" Brock said. He looked at her with love in

his eyes — just as he did when he set eyes on any pretty girl.

"And Plusle, too!" Max said.

Ash remembered Solana. They had helped the Pokémon Ranger rescue an injured Celebi once.

Brock raced toward Solana. "I'm Brock, don't you remember? I've missed you so much!"

Solana looked at him sternly. "Not now, Brock, please," she said. "Right now, we've got to help all those Pokémon!"

Deoxys Appears

Plusle jumped to the ground. Solana turned her Capture Styler on the flock of Altaria and Swablu. The device scanned the Pokémon. The results showed up on the small screen.

"That one should work," she said, eyeing one of the Altaria.

She closed the screen and pointed the device at the Altaria. A small object that looked like a metal top flew out of the styler. It flew around the Altaria, circling it with white light. Altaria gasped, confused.

"Hiyaaaaa!" Solana cried. She moved the Capture Styler in a circle. The light grew brighter

and brighter. A long antenna extended from the Capture Styler. Solana pointed it right at Altaria.

The light formed a tight band around Altaria's body, then disappeared.

"Capture complete!" Solana said triumphantly. "Altaria, use Refresh!"

A bright light washed over Altaria's body. It was no longer confused.

"Now fly back to your friends and take the lead!" Solana told the Pokémon.

Altaria flew off with a cry. It circled the confused flock. Then it flew off toward the mountains once again.

The Altaria and Swablu stopped flying in circles. They followed the Altaria.

Ash and his friends climbed up the cliff to watch. Ash knew that when a Pokémon Ranger used a Capture Styler, the Pokémon wasn't captured forever. That's why Altaria was able to fly away.

"Wow, it's working!" Max said. "Look at them go!"

Solana smiled at a job well done. She lowered her Capture Styler. Plusle jumped back onto her shoulder.

"Solana, what are you doing here?" Ash asked.

"Working," the Pokémon Ranger replied. "We've been detecting unusual geomagnetic activity."

"Geomagnetic activity?" May asked.

"It's similar to the magnetic forces given off by the Earth, but it's extremely chaotic," Solana explained.

"Do you think that explains what was wrong with the Altaria?" Brock asked.

Solana nodded. "I do, since Altaria use geomagnetic fields as they move from place to place. Any disturbance would throw them way off."

"Also, my Pikachu was acting strange," Ash pointed out.

"Electric-type Pokémon are affected by this

as well," Solana said. "That would explain the aurora that appeared in the sky."

"And our Poké Balls and PokéNav weren't working at all," Max added. "Why does your Capture Styler seem to be working just fine?"

"Pokémon Rangers have to be able to perform their duties in the most extreme environments," Solana told him. "So we hermetically seal our equipment. That way we're sure it'll always work, no matter what."

Max was impressed. "Wow! You Pokémon Rangers get all the coolest stuff."

"Pika! Pika!"

Pikachu gave a warning cry. It pointed toward the sky.

A shimmering blue aurora appeared. A dark blue ball of light formed inside it. The ball glowed in shades of red and purple.

A Pokémon emerged from the light. Two eyes shone from its blue face. It didn't have a nose or

mouth. Its long body was red, and it had two sets of arms that extended out like long ropes. The top set of arms was red, and the bottom set was blue.

"It's Deoxys!" Max cried.

Max stared, amazed at Deoxys. The Pokémon seemed to be gazing right into his eyes.

An image flashed into Max's mind. He saw the darkness of outer space, dotted with masses of bright stars. Max gasped. Was Deoxys sending him the image?

"Hmm, I wonder," Solana said softly.

Deoxys flew back up into the aurora. It disappeared, and the aurora vanished from the sky.

"It's gone!" Ash said.

12

"We've got to hurry," Solana said urgently. "There's a Pokémon Center very close to here."

The Pokémon Center was nestled at the foot of the mountains. Every Pokémon Center was run by a Nurse Joy, and this one was no different. Her pink hair matched the pink nurse's uniform she wore.

"Nurse Joy, how is your computer system working?" Solana asked.

"Not good," Nurse Joy replied. "It won't even boot up! It has to be the geomagnetic disturbance."

"You should know we saw a Deoxys out there," Solana told her.

Nurse Joy's eyes widened. Deoxys was a very rare Pokémon. "That would explain all the electrical problems."

"But what would Deoxys be doing here?" Ash wondered.

"This isn't the first time," Solana said. "There is a report by Professor Lund, a Pokémon researcher. Deoxys made an appearance in

Larousse City. He said Deoxys came here on a meteorite."

"Ten years ago, a meteorite crashed somewhere in the mountains!" Nurse Joy said.

Ash and his friends gasped. Could that meteorite have contained Deoxys?

"Then we need to find out where the meteorite actually landed," Solana said. "Do you have the location?"

"Yes! I've got the map. Hold on," Nurse Joy said.

Nurse Joy hurried off. Max turned to Solana.

"Can I go with you? Please?" he begged.

"What are you talking about?" May asked.

"May, I've got to see Deoxys again," Max said. He couldn't explain it, exactly, but he had a strange feeling. A feeling that Deoxys was trying to tell him something.

May frowned. "But that could be dangerous!"

"I know, but I have to go," Max pleaded. "To tell the truth, I'm not sure why right now."

Solana looked at him kindly. "I know. Your feelings are strong," she said. "But we need to do a thorough investigation now, and that kind of work should be left to the Pokémon Rangers."

"Please!" Max begged.

"Since this kind of work can be extremely dangerous, I'm asking all of you to wait here," Solana said.

Ash nodded. "Sure!"

Nurse Joy came back with a piece of paper. She handed it to Solana. "Here, this shows you where the meteorite landed."

"Thanks, Nurse Joy!" Solana said.

She and her Plusle hurried out of the Pokémon Center. Max sadly watched them go.

Solana was right. A powerful Pokémon like Deoxys could be very dangerous.

But he had to see Deoxys again . . . no matter what!

Psycho Boost!

Solana followed the map. She traveled into the woods. The trail led to the mouth of a cave carved into the mountainside.

Plusle grimaced and squeaked from its perch on Solana's shoulder.

"You're feeling the geomagnetic waves, aren't you?" Solana asked. "It all seems to be coming from this cave."

Solana was about to step into the cave when she heard a rustling sound behind her. She turned.

"All right. You come out of there, Max!" she said sternly.

Max appeared from behind a bush. "I know you said to stay put, but I've just got to see Deoxys!"

Solana shook her head. "Kids with commitment."

Ash, May, and Max came running down the trail.

"Hey, there they are!" Ash cried.

"Max, what are you doing?" May scolded. "Solana told you not to come here!"

"Yeah, then what are *you* guys doing here?" Max asked.

Solana's eyes narrowed. "Good question!"

Ash laughed. "Uh, I guess we wanted to come, too."

Sparks crackled on Pikachu's cheeks. Ash looked at Pikachu with concern.

Solana knew they would follow her, no matter what. She sighed. "If I let you all come along, will you stay out of trouble?"

"Of course!" everyone replied at once.

Solana took a small device from her jacket

pocket. "We'll use this to measure the geomagnetic waves in the cave. Keep an eye on this for me!"

Brock quickly grabbed it. "I'd love to!"

They entered the cave. Solana led the group, using a flashlight to show the way. Max walked in front of her.

They walked for a little while, when Brock let out a surprised gasp. "The geomagnetic disturbance has disappeared," he said. "I've got a normal reading!"

"Pikachu, how do you feel?" Ash asked.

"Pika!" Pikachu said happily. Its cheeks had stopped sparking.

Plusle smiled on Solana's shoulder.

"Wow, Plusle looks a lot better, too," May remarked.

Solana looked thoughtful. "I'm fairly sure this condition is only temporary," she said. "For now, we'll just have to watch out!"

Max couldn't wait to find Deoxys. He ran

ahead of the group. He turned a corner in the cave — and saw a Pokémon up ahead.

"Look! A Miltank!" Max cried.

Miltank looked surprised to see humans in the cave. The pink Pokémon had a round, fat body. It had black hooves, black ears, and tiny white horns on top of its head. There was an udder on its belly.

Solana and the others caught up.

"Perfect timing!" Solana said. She pointed her Capture Styler at the Miltank. "Capture on!"

The spinning top flew out of the Capture Styler. It flew around Miltank. Solana cried out as she waved the styler around and around in a circle.

The light swirled faster and faster around Miltank. It tightened around Miltank's body. Then a white light washed over the Pokémon.

"Capture complete!" Solana said proudly. "Miltank, please follow me!"

"But what are you going to do?" May asked.

"I think Miltank just might be able to help us out," Solana said.

They walked on. The cave grew brighter. Max looked up to see a hole in the cave where the meteorite had crashed through. Below it was a huge, round rock. Half of the rock was buried under the floor of the cave.

"This has to be the meteorite we're looking for!" Solana said.

"It's huge!" Ash cried.

"I wonder if that means Deoxys is nearby?" Brock mused.

Max decided to find out. "Hey, Deoxys. It's Max!" he called out.

Suddenly, Ash cried out. Pikachu's cheeks began to spark with electricity again. The walls of the cave started to rumble. Brock checked the device.

"I'm picking up a reading again!" he said.

A shimmering white light appeared right above the meteorite. A core of purple and red

light appeared inside. The head of Deoxys appeared inside the light. Then the Pokémon slowly emerged from the light. It hovered in the air above the meteorite.

"Pika! Pika!" Pikachu cried out as its electric power went out of control.

Plusle's red ears drooped. The little Pokémon whimpered. "You, too?" Solana asked, worried.

Deoxys changed Forme in front of their eyes. Its chest changed color from red to gray, and the jewel on its chest glowed purple. Blue spikes jutted out from its legs, and three red spikes formed on its head.

Deoxys brought its four arms together in front of its body. A ball of swirling rainbow light formed at the tips of its arms.

Solana knew what was coming. "It's Psycho Boost!" she cried.

The ball of light grew bigger and bigger. Then Deoxys hurled it toward the group of friends.

Everyone jumped out of the way of the powerful attack.

Bam! The Psycho Boost attack exploded against the cave wall, sending chips of rock flying everywhere.

The explosion knocked Ash to the ground. He struggled to sit up.

"Pikachu, use Thunderbolt!" he yelled.

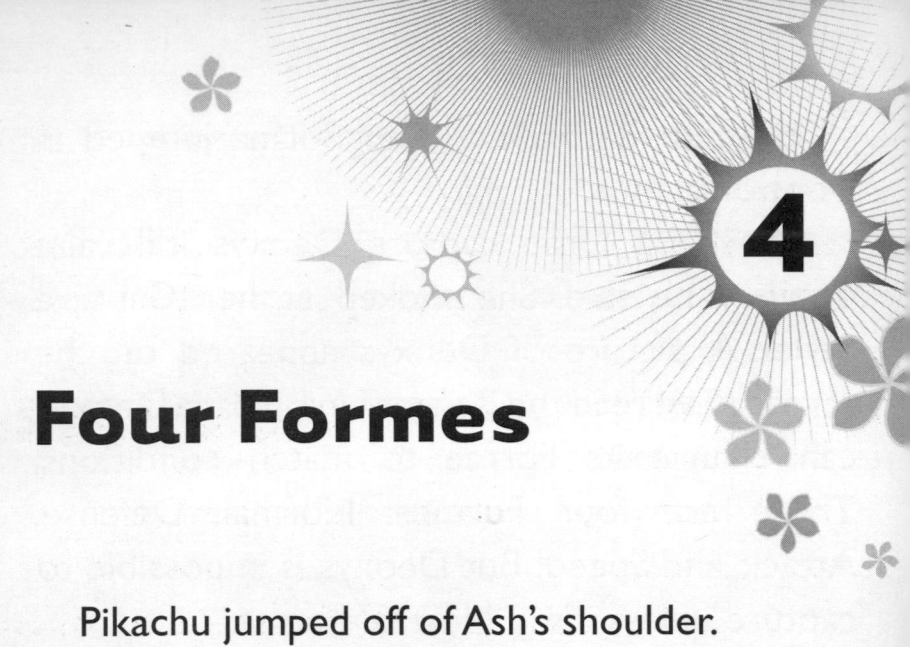

Four Formes

Pikachu jumped off of Ash's shoulder. *"Piiiiiikaaaaaaaaa!"*

A blazing yellow lightning bolt zoomed across the cave. Deoxys changed its Forme again. The blue spikes on its legs turned into blue circles. Its head took on the shape of a red helmet. Its chest changed so it looked like it was protected with red armor. And its arms became wide and flat.

Deoxys curled its body into a ball. A protective bubble of light appeared around it. The lightning bolt hit the bubble, and then vaporized without harming Deoxys.

Pikachu ran back to Ash. Solana jumped in front of them.

"Maybe if I can capture Deoxys it'll calm down," she said. She looked at her Capture Styler. A picture of Deoxys appeared on the screen. "I've read the Ranger Union data. Deoxys can change its Forme to match conditions. There are four Formes: Normal, Defense, Attack, and Speed! But Deoxys is impossible to capture unless it's in Normal Forme."

Ash frowned. He had seen Deoxys change its Forme in the blink of an eye. If what Solana said was true, Deoxys wouldn't be easy to capture. But it was worth a try.

"So we keep watching until it's in Normal Forme, and then . . . wham!" Ash said.

As he spoke, Deoxys was already transforming.

"Like now!" Solana cried. "Capture on!"

She pointed the Capture Styler at Deoxys. The spinning top flew out. But Deoxys quickly

changed Forme before the top reached it. Its body shape became sleek, and now it was gray. The helmet on its head transformed to a long fin that extended behind it. Its four arms became just two: one red and one blue.

As soon as it changed Forme, Deoxys quickly moved out of the way.

"That must be Speed Forme!" Brock guessed.

Deoxys hovered in front of them once more, still in Speed Forme. A strange sound came from Deoxys.

"It's talking," Max said. But he didn't understand anything Deoxys was saying.

Deoxys transormed back into Normal Forme before their eyes. Solana didn't hesitate. She activated the Capture Styler once more.

"Capture on!" she yelled.

A circle of light enclosed Deoxys this time. But the Pokémon changed once again. It was back in Defense Forme. It curled its body up into a ball.

A white light formed around Deoxys. The light exploded, canceling the effect of the Capture Styler.

Solana stared at Deoxys, shocked. She wasn't sure what to do.

Deoxys made more strange sounds. Max looked into its eyes.

"I wish I knew what it was saying," he said.

Deoxys changed into Attack Forme or again and started to charge up another Psycho Boost.

"Run!" Ash yelled.

Bam! This attack was even more powerful than the last. The force of the explosion sent everyone tumbling around the cave.

A short distance away, Team Rocket watched the attack from behind a rock. The trio of Pokémon thieves was always following Ash around, trying to steal Pikachu for their boss. Now they had an even better Pokémon to poach — Deoxys!

"Nice attack!" said Jessie, a young woman with long red hair.

"Hey, something's wrong," said Meowth. Team Rocket's talking Pokémon was short and furry. It had big eyes, whiskers, and pointy ears. Besides being able to talk, Meowth understood the language of other Pokémon. "Deoxys is in some kind of pain."

"...really?" asked James, Jessie's blue-haired partner in crime.

"...Mime?" repeated Mime Jr. James's tiny pink Pokémon sat on his back. Mime Jr. had a round red nose. The top of its head looked like a pointed blue hat with a white pom-pom on top. Ash and his friends didn't know they were being watched. They slowly got to their feet. Luckily, no one had been hurt by the Psycho Boost.

Deoxys began to fly around the cave.

"Something's really wrong with that Deoxys!" Max said. He wasn't sure how he knew — he just knew.

Deoxys suddenly stopped flying. Its body curled up as though it was in pain.

"Let's check it out, Max," Solana said. She flipped open a screen on her Capture Styler. She pointed the Styler at Deoxys. But she wasn't trying to capture it now. The Capture Styler could analyze the Pokémon. It would show Solana if Deoxys was healthy or sick.

"Oh, no!" she said, as the data flashed on the screen. "Deoxys is in a terrible amount of pain. But I can't pinpoint the cause of it."

"We've got to do something to help," Max urged.

"Of course we will!" Solana said confidently. "That's why I captured Miltank. Quick, Miltank. Use Heal Bell, now!"

Miltank jumped toward the meteorite. It pointed its long tail at Deoxys. The round ball on the end of the tail turned blue. A beautiful, sparkling light shone from the tail. The light grew bigger and bigger until it filled the whole

cave. The sound of soothing chimes echoed off of the rocks.

The light washed over Deoxys. The Pokémon straightened out its body. Deoxys looked calm and peaceful.

"It's working!" Solana said. "The geomagnetic levels are down. Miltank, thanks a lot!"

She closed the screen on her Styler. This was the perfect time to capture Deoxys.

Solana activated the Capture Styler once more. The light encircled Deoxys. She swung the Styler around and around. She was so close. . . .

Deoxys changed into Defense Forme at the last second. The capture didn't work.

"But why?" Solana wondered.

Those weird sounds came from Deoxys again.

"Deoxys is still trying to talk," Max said. He knew that Deoxys had something important to say. The Pokémon didn't want to be captured.

Deoxys changed into Attack Forme again. It prepared another Psycho Boost. The energy ball it created was twice as big as the last one.

"Out of the way!" Solana yelled.

Deoxys Speaks

The huge blast sent everyone flying. Miltank ran away in terror.

Suddenly three figures appeared on top of the meteorite.

"Prepare for trouble. It's all about us!" said Jessie.

"And make it double, no muss, no fuss!" said James.

Jessie grinned. "Wherever there's peace in the universe . . ."

". . . Team Rocket," said James.

". . . will be there," said Meowth.

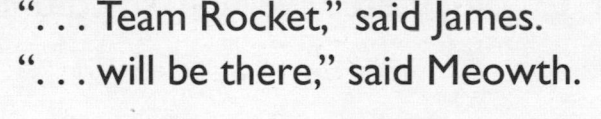

"To make everything worse!" they all finished together.

"*Mime!*" chimed in Mime Jr.

Jessie's big blue Pokémon got into the act, too. "*Wobbuffet!*"

"Team Rocket!" Ash cried.

"You're lookin' at Deoxys' new family!" Meowth told him.

Deoxys floated up behind Team Rocket. Jessie and James saw the Pokémon right away. They ran away screaming, followed by Mime Jr. and Wobbuffet.

Meowth turned around.

"Yipes!" Meowth said. "Say something already!"

Deoxys answered with the strange machine noise.

"I know you're feelin' bad, but why?" Meowth asked.

Max ran to the meteorite. He started to climb up.

"Max, no!" May cried. "You're gonna get yourself hurt!"

"Sorry, guys," Max said. "I've just gotta get up there and try to figure out why Deoxys is in so much pain!"

Max reached the top. He stood next to Meowth.

"Hey, twerp," Meowth said. "So what do you want?"

"Do you know what Deoxys is trying to say?" Max asked.

"Sorry, but I don't understand space lingo," Meowth replied.

Deoxys seemed to study Meowth and Max for a moment. A soft, green glow lit up its body. The glow expanded, turning into a dome of green light.

The dome covered Deoxys, Max, Meowth, and the meteorite below them.

"Whoa, it's using Safeguard," Brock realized.

Ash threw his body against the bubble. He bounced right off of it with a groan.

Jessie pounded on the bubble with her fists. "Let Meowth go!" she yelled. James joined in, kicking the bubble. But it would not break.

Max wasn't scared at all.

"Come on, Deoxys. Tell us what you're thinking, please," Max said.

"Yeah, you're a sharp Pokémon," said Meowth.

Suddenly, Meowth's body began to shake and twist. Then a sudden calm came over Meowth. A white light shone in its eyes.

"*I'm scared,*" Meowth said. But the voice was not Meowth's voice!

Meowth's body floated off of the meteorite. It hung in the air next to Deoxys.

Max understood. Deoxys was using Meowth to communicate.

"Tell me what you're scared of," Max said.

"*You'll listen to me?*" Deoxys asked, through Meowth's body.

"My name's Max, and I want to hear everything you have to say," Max said.

Deoxys nodded. It looked into Max's eyes. A vision came into Max's head, just like it had on the mountain. He saw a meteoroid flying through space. But he could also *feel* what it was like. A cold, quiet feeling swept over his body.

"Is that how cold it was when you were flying through space?" Max asked.

"*Yes,*" Deoxys said. "*I was very cold. And scared.*"

"Of course you were," Max said. "That's too much for anyone."

Now Max's body began to float, too. Deoxys, Meowth, and Max floated up, toward the hole in the ceiling of the cave.

"*So cold,*" Deoxys said. "*So scared. And so alone.*"

Then they all disappeared.

Deoxys' Story

Everyone went back to the Pokémon Center. They needed to form a plan.

"Please help us!" James begged.

"Save our dear Meowth!" Jessie pleaded.

Tears streamed down their cheeks. Pikachu ran up to James and held out its paws in friendship.

"We'll help you," Ash said. Team Rocket always caused a lot of trouble. But he hated to see anyone in danger — even Meowth. Besides, they had to save Max!

"Then we'll call a truce!" Jessie said happily.

Solana ran up to the group. "I sent a question to Ranger Base, and I just received a reply. Check this out. Have you ever heard of a solar wind?"

"Don't think so," Ash said.

"It's the sun's wind," Solana explained. "Plasma comes from the sun and bathes our planet. We're entering a cycle when sun spots are growing larger. They're black spots on the sun that are cooler areas on the sun's surface. They increase and decrease in size every ten years. When sun spots get larger, the solar winds get stronger."

Solana held up her Capture Styler so everyone could see the screen. "I had the Ranger Base map out the pattern of the solar winds. It's the exact same pattern as the geomagnetic disturbances."

"So does that mean the solar winds are causing the geomagnetic mayhem?" James asked.

Solana shook her head. "No. According to the Ranger Base, the center of the disturbance is in the cave."

"You sure?" Brock asked.

Solana nodded. "We've got to go back there. That's where we'll find all of our answers."

Max opened his eyes. When Deoxys carried Meowth and Max out of the cave, a weird feeling had come over him. He felt sleepy. But now he was awake.

Max looked around. He was still floating, but he definitely wasn't in the cave anymore. He was in a white bubble. Strange, colorful shapes floated around him. The shapes reminded him of macaroni.

Meowth floated in the bubble, too.

"Hey Meowth, where are we?" Max asked.

"I don't know." Meowth said. His normal voice was back.

"Wow, Meowth, you sound normal again," Max said.

Meowth looked puzzled. "What do you mean?"

"Don't you remember what happened?" Max asked.

"Nah . . ." Meowth answered. But before Max could explain, Deoxys appeared in the bubble.

Meowth hugged Max, afraid. "That big Pokémon's back!"

"Deoxys, where are we?" Max asked.

Meowth's body began to glow with white light again. The Pokémon floated out of Max's arms. It hung in the air next to Deoxys. Meowth's eyes glowed white, too.

Deoxys is using Meowth again, Max realized.

"*I will use this one to communicate with you,*" Deoxys said. Just like before, its voice came

from Meowth's body. *"Don't worry. This one will not be harmed."*

"Okay," Max said. "So where is this?"

"It's my room," Deoxys answered.

Max was confused. "But I thought you were living in that cave?"

"I hate that cave! My room is right . . . here," Deoxys answered. It lowered its head and sighed.

"Okay," Max said. "So, did you come here from outer space? Did that meteor bring you here?"

"Yes," Deoxys answered. *"I was all alone. It was small, and I was so very cold."*

Max listened, amazed, as Deoxys told its story.

"There was no sound in space," Deoxys began. *"All I wanted to do was hear another voice. Then, after a very long time, I heard a crash! The meteorite landed on this planet. I was so happy. I thought someone would come to meet me. I would hear a voice. I would have a friend.*

"*But no one came,*" Deoxys went on. "*I thought I had landed on an empty planet. After a while, I felt much too frightened to come out of the cave. I have been alone ever since.*"

"That's awful," Max said. "But you're not alone, Deoxys. I'm here with you. And there are lots of Pokémon on this planet, too!"

Deoxys raised its head. "*Why, that's true!*"

"That's right," Max said. He smiled.

He knew why Deoxys was sad. Now maybe they could help it! But first, they had to find out why Deoxys was in so much pain.

Max tried to look outside the bubble. All he could see were the weird shapes.

Solana will find an answer, Max said to himself. *After all, she's a Pokémon Ranger!*

The Source of the Trouble

Solana led the others through the cave once again. This time, Nurse Joy came with them. No one was sure where Deoxys had taken Max and Meowth.

"Why don't we have the Pokémon help us out?" Brock suggested.

"Sounds good!" Ash agreed.

Brock brought out a Poké Ball. "Marshtomp, come on out!"

A blue Pokémon came out of the Poké Ball. Marshtomp's feet looked like flat fins. A black fin grew on top of its head. It had two more fins on its tail, and its belly was orange.

"Combusken, you too!" May cried.

Combusken came out of May's Poké Ball. It was yellow and orange, with an orange crest on top of its head. It had a small beak, and eyes that burned with orange fire.

"Swellow and Sceptile, I need your help!" Ash yelled.

Swellow flew out of one of Ash's Poké Balls. The Flying-type Pokémon had a white belly and blue wings. Its neck and face were red. Two sharp tail feathers grew from its back.

Sceptile was a green Grass-type Pokémon almost as tall as Brock. Two sharp, spiky leaves grew from its arms. Its tail looked like a leafy tree branch. Yellow, orb-shaped pods grew on its back.

"Okay," Ash cried. "I want you guys to split up and find Max and Meowth."

The Pokémon quickly took off in different directions. They were just out of sight when the whole cave began to rumble.

Brock checked the screen of the measuring device. "We've got a geomagnetic disturbance!" he announced.

Pikachu and Plusle both moaned. The disturbance was really affecting them. Ash took his backpack off of his shoulders.

"Hop in here," he told Pikachu.

"*Pika!*" Pikachu said gratefully.

"Let me take Plusle," Nurse Joy offered.

"That's a big help. Thank you!" Solana said.

They hurried through the cave. Up ahead, they saw Marshtomp, Combusken, Sceptile, and Swellow. They had all arrived in the same place.

Right in front of the meteorite.

"Did you find anything?" Ash asked.

Combusken pointed to the meteorite. A white bubble floated above it. Ash could see Meowth, Max, and Deoxys inside! Deoxys was doubled over in pain.

"It's Max!" May cried.

"And Meowth!" Jessie said happily.

"They must be stuck in a space that Deoxys created," Solana guessed.

Deoxys groaned and burst through the bubble. It landed on top of the meteorite.

"No, Deoxys!" Max yelled.

Deoxys tried to talk. But all anyone could hear were the strange noises it made.

"What's Deoxys saying?" Jessie wondered.

"Sorry, I don't do space talk!" James answered frantically.

Pikachu's cheeks began to spark violently. Then the meteorite started to spark, too. Waves of electricity sizzled on its surface.

"What's that?" Ash asked.

Brock checked the measuring device. The geomagnetic reading was out of control. The machine began to sizzle and smoke. Brock cried out and dropped it.

"The meteorite did that," Brock said. "That's a massive energy build up."

Solana suddenly knew what was happening. "So that's it!" she cried. "The meteorite has been affected by the solar winds, not Deoxys! The meteorite is causing all of the geomagnetic disturbances!"

Deoxys nodded. Someone finally understood.

Solana took a reading with her Capture Styler. The meteorite crackled with intense electric power.

"It's extremely dangerous in here. Get out at once!" Solana cried.

Everyone turned and ran. But they were too late.

A huge blast of energy exploded right behind them!

Capture On!

The tremendous force of the blast pushed them all out of the cave. They slammed into the dirt. Rocks and debris fell all around them.

Ash was sprawled face-down on the ground. He looked up to see Sceptile standing over him concerned. Pikachu stood next to his head.

"*Pika pika?*" Pikachu asked.

"I'm okay," he told his Pokémon. He slowly sat up and looked around.

Everyone looked beaten up. But they were all in one piece.

"We landed in a valley," Solana said, rising to her feet. She looked over at the mountain.

Beams of light shot out of the hole in the top of the cave.

"The energy from the meteorite is out of control!" she said. "It all makes sense now. Researchers think that Deoxys are formed in the core of a meteor. It happens when the solar winds combine with the meteor's energy. But now that energy is causing disturbances, and it's affecting Deoxys very strongly."

"That's just so sad," Nurse Joy remarked. "The meteor that was supposed to be its cradle is actually causing it pain."

"That must be what Deoxys was trying to tell us all along!" May realized.

A clap of thunder rocked the valley. Ash looked into the sky. Threatening rain clouds appeared, streaked with jagged lightning.

"The energy from the meteorite is starting to lower the air pressure," Solana said, checking her data. "This could be bad news for the whole area."

"*Sceptile!*" Ash's Pokémon cried.

Everyone turned toward Sceptile. It pointed toward the mountain, where Deoxys had suddenly appeared. Max and Meowth floated behind it in the white bubble.

"Okay, I need everyone's help," Solana said. "I need to capture Deoxys and use Recover on it. That may be the only way to heal it."

"Right!" everyone agreed.

"Because I can only capture Deoxys in its Normal Forme, I need you and your Pokémon to keep Deoxys restrained!" Solana explained. "That way, when it's finally in Normal Forme, I'll be able to capture Deoxys once and for all."

"You've got it!" Ash said, clenching his fist. "Let's do it, guys!"

Deoxys changed into its Attack Forme. It was gearing up for another Psycho Boost.

"Now Sceptile! Bullet Seed, go!" Ash yelled.

Sceptile opened its mouth and shot a barrage of glowing seeds at the swirling ball of light.

"Combusken, use Flamethrower!" May cried.

May's Pokémon opened its beak and let loose with a wave of flame.

"Marshtomp, Water Gun! Let's go!" Brock called out.

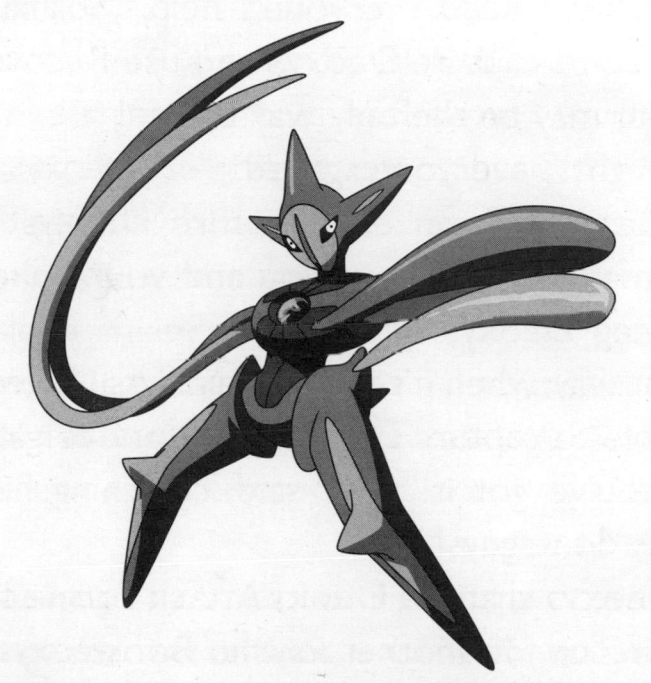

A powerful stream of water spun from Marshstomp's mouth. Seed, fire, and water all struck the Psycho Boost.

But the ball of rainbow light kept coming. Everyone had to dodge out of the way.

Blam! The Psycho Boost exploded in the dirt.

"Deoxys, please stop!" Nurse Joy pleaded. "Can't you see these people are just trying to help you?"

Deoxys didn't listen. *Blam! Blam!* It hurled two more Psycho Boosts at the ground.

Solana tried to get a lock on Deoxys with her Capture Styler. Deoxys changed into Speed Forme. It flew back and forth across the sky, dodging her.

"Sceptile, do Bullet Seed again!" Ash called out.

Sceptile obeyed. Another round of glowing seeds shot from its mouth. But Deoxys easily dodged them.

"Swellow, follow Deoxys!" Ash ordered.

Swellow flew up into the sky. Deoxys was fast, but Swellow could keep up. Soon Ash's Pokémon was just a wing's width away from Deoxys.

"Aerial Ace now!" Ash yelled.

Swellow slammed into Deoxys. Deoxys reeled from the blow, then quickly flew away again.

"Good work! Swellow, use Quick Attack!" Ash cried out.

Swellow's body glowed with light as it zoomed toward Deoxys with amazing speed. But Deoxys was ready. This time, it dodged the attack.

Brock shook his head. "Swellow will never catch up to it."

Now Deoxys flew after Swellow, ready to attack.

"Swellow, use Aerial Ace to dodge!" Ash called out.

Swellow's body glowed again. But it wasn't fast enough to avoid Deoxys.

Slam! Deoxys collided with Swellow in mid-air.

"*Swell! Swell!*" the Pokémon cried. It hurtled through the air and landed at Ash's feet.

Ash knelt by his Pokémon's side. "Swellow, are you okay?"

The brewing storm quickly grew worse. Lightning streaked the sky. The thunderclaps came every few seconds.

A wicked wind blew up. It rocked the bubble holding Max and Meowth.

"Help!" Max cried.

Jessie, James, and May ran toward the bubble. But they didn't get far. Loud explosions rocked the valley. Rays of yellow energy shot up all throughout the woods.

"It looks like the energy has started a chain reaction!" Solana realized.

In the sky, Deoxys groaned.

"The energy from the meteorite must really hurt!" Brock remarked.

"Keep watching!" Solana told him. "We have to catch Deoxys when it's in Normal Forme!"

Jessie, James, and May finally reached the bubble. It was getting smaller and smaller. Soon Max and Meowth would be trapped inside it forever!

"May, help me!" Max yelled.

May reached up and grabbed on to her brother's leg. She pulled with all of her might. Max tumbled onto the ground next to her.

Jessie and James reached in and grabbed Meowth. They pulled the Pokémon out just as the bubble collapsed into itself.

"You're back!" Jessie and James cried happily.

Meowth sobbed. "No place like home! That movie's right!"

Above them, Deoxys was doubled over in pain once again. Ash saw his chance.

"Sceptile, now!" Ash cried.

Sceptile jumped up and wrapped its body around Deoxys. Deoxys struggled, but Sceptile held on. Deoxys couldn't change into its Defense Forme.

"Sceptile, Solar Beam!" Ash cried.

The orbs on Sceptile's back began to glow as it gathered energy for the powerful attack. Sceptile opened its mouth. A huge beam of energy as powerful as the sun slammed into Deoxys.

Not even Deoxys could withstand a Solar Beam attack from such close range. The blast sent Deoxys slamming into the mountainside. It automatically reverted to its Normal Forme.

"Capture on!" Solana said quickly. She aimed the Capture Styler at Deoxys. The metal top spun out. It circled the Pokémon. A ring of white light appeared around it.

"Hiiyaaaa!" Solana cried. She spun the Styler around and around. The ring of light grew stronger. Deoxys tried to resist. But the light was too strong. It circled around Deoxys' waist.

Then it disappeared.

"Capture complete!" Solana cried out.

Deoxys to the Rescue

"Now, Deoxys, Recover!" Solana called out.

A yellow light flowed over Deoxys' body. The Pokémon stretched out its long limbs. The light faded, and Deoxys looked down at Solana.

Solana smiled. "Looks like it worked!"

Max ran up, followed by May and Team Rocket. He cried out happily when he saw Deoxys.

"Deoxys!"

Max ran toward the Pokémon. But he couldn't get far. Huge chunks of rock flew out of the hole in the cave. The meteorite's energy was completely out of control.

"We've got to get out of here!" Solana warned.

Deoxys flew over the hole. A blue bubble formed around its body.

"What's that?" Ash asked.

"It's a Safeguard," Solana said.

The bubble seemed to glow from within. There was a rumbling sound, and a huge explosion erupted from the meteorite. A massive cloud of smoke and debris flew out of the hole.

But the bubble absorbed everything. The smoke disappeared. The strong winds died down. The rain clouds vanished from the sky.

The bubble faded, leaving Deoxys floating peacefully in the air.

"*Plus!*" Solana's Pokémon gave a happy cry.

"Look at your Plusle now," Nurse Joy said, smiling.

Pikachu felt better, too. "*Pikachu!*"

Max looked up at Deoxys. "Thanks," he said. "You ended up rescuing every one of us!"

Deoxys nodded. Meowth's eyes began to glow once more. It floated up in front of Deoxys.

"*Of course,*" Deoxys replied. "*You're my friend.*"

"And you're mine," Max told him. "What are you going to do now?"

"*I wish to see more of this planet of yours,*" Deoxys answered. "*There are many places to visit, and many wonderful Pokémon, as you know.*"

"I know!" Max said, smiling. "Well, I'll see you later."

Deoxys released Meowth. Team Rocket's Pokémon gently floated to the ground.

"Take care! You promise?" Max asked.

Deoxys responded in its own language. It floated up into the sky. Then it swirled through the white fluffy clouds, and disappeared.

"Wonder what Deoxys just said?" Ash asked.

Max grinned. "Easy. Deoxys just promised, that's all."

"Of course!" May agreed.

Then Ash noticed something. "Hey!" he cried, pointing.

A beautiful aurora lit up the sky. Blue and purple lights shimmered like crystals. Then they slowly faded away.

Solana talked into her Capture Styler. "This is Solana here. Mission complete!"

Max kept staring up into the sky. He was happy that he could help Deoxys.

And maybe, someday, they would meet again.